AMERICAN ELVES - THE YANKOOS

THE YANKOOS

AND

THE OAK-HICKORY FOREST ECOLOGY

BOOK THREE

By Robert Frieders, Ph.D.

One of a Yankoo Series of Books

COVER: Finian, the yankoo naturalist, examines the Pink Lady's-slipper orchid. This orchid, found in the forest, is also called the Moccasin Flower.

Yankoo Publishing Co.

AMERICAN ELVES - THE YANKOOS

THE YANKOOS

AND

THE OAK-HICKORY FOREST ECOLOGY

BOOK THREE

By Robert Frieders, Ph.D.

All photographs and line drawings by the author

Published by: The Yankoo Publishing Co.
10616 W. Cameo Drive
Sun City, AZ 85351-2708

First Printing 1994

Printed in the United States of America

Library of Congress Catalog Card Number 93-61530

ISBN 0-9639284-2-2 $7.95 Soft cover 6x9

Acknowledgments

Dottie and I wish to thank our friends who have helped make this book a reality:

Our Consultant   **- Dr. Mamie Ross**

Our Editor   **- Professor Marge Edwards**

Our Computer Editor   **- Lorraine Glicksman**

We are all proud of this book on the plant and animal life of the Oak-Hickory Forest. The American elves, the yankoos, should provide young readers with an interesting adventure as they learn about life in the forest.

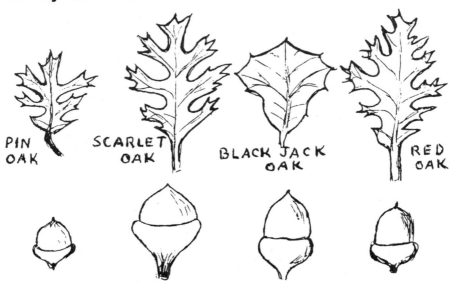

PIN OAK   SCARLET OAK   BLACK JACK OAK   RED OAK

Table of Contents

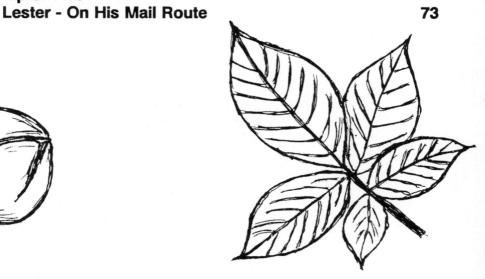

CHAPTER ONE

LESTER - ON HIS MAIL ROUTE

Lester crosses a small brook on his way to Bruno, the baker. The woods alongside this brook are quite wet. The water flows in this brook all year.

Hello, my friend! I am Lester the yankoo mailman. I'm glad to have you go with me on my mail route. Along the way, we will undoubtedly come across many interesting plants and animals of our forest. We will also meet some of our forest yankoos. So - let's "hit the mail trail" through the forest.

Now, let me look in my mail pouch. Bruno is the next yankoo on my mail route. But, I wonder, do I have a letter for him today? Oh, yes, I do indeed have a letter for Bruno.

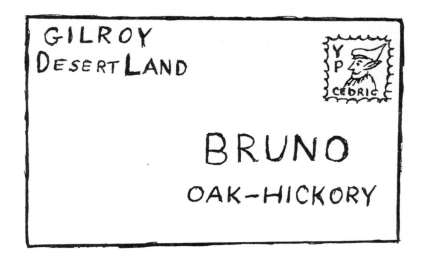

Gilroy has written to him. Gilroy was a Breton. He lived in the part of France called Brittany. When Gilroy came over, he headed west. He is one of our oldest yankoos out there in the Desert Land. Gilroy grows citrus trees - oranges, grapefruits and lemons. He supplies the desert yankoos with their citrus fruits.

Bruno gave me a picture of Gilroy. It should be in my mail pouch. Yes, here it is.

Notice Gilroy has picked a bag of oranges from this tree. Now, he is looking at the flowers on the tree. That tree, my friend, has mature oranges on it. At the same time, it also has flowers for next year's crop of oranges. Very few trees have both flowers and fruit at the same time.

On our way, we go to Bruno's house. You will like Bruno, my friend. All the yankoos like Bruno. Bruno is the yankoo baker. He bakes delicious cookies, cakes, and pies. He might just have something for us. We shall see what he has baked today.

Sh! Sh! Be very quiet, my friend. Up ahead is a Red Fox. Look over there to your left. Do you see it? It is in front of those tree trunks.

I do believe that fox is trailing an animal. Animals, you know, leave an odor or scent trail as they move through the forest. A fox is able to pick up these odor trails.

Yes, that Red Fox is following a scent trail. See how its head goes down every so often to the ground as it moves along? Its nose is not too far from the ground. It is picking up the scent of an animal that has left an odor trail.

Down goes the head again. Yes, it is definitely on the trail of an animal.

You know, my friend, that scent or odor trail tells the fox many things. Most important, it indicates the path the animal is taking.

In addition, the odor tells the fox what animal is making the trail.

The scent or odor trail gives the fox still more information. As an animal passes a spot, it leaves a very strong scent there. As time elapses, the scent gets weaker and weaker. So, a strong scent tells the fox that the animal is just ahead. A weak scent tells the fox that the animal passed some time ago. So, you can see, my friend, that Red Fox knows a lot about the animal it is tracking.

This Red Fox and its mate have set up their territory. This is their part of the forest. No other Red Fox is welcome in this area. They mark their territory. At certain spots around this area, they urinate. These scent spots warn other Red Foxes to keep out. If another Red Fox did come into the territory, it would be driven out. The pair update the scent spots at regular intervals.

This fox has a den on the side of a nearby slope. The pair have taken over an old Ground Hog den. The opening to the den is partly covered by a large bush.

The other day I was over by the den. I saw the fox come out of the opening, and I made a sketch of it. It should be here in my mail pouch. Yes, here it is.

See the small opening to the den. It is amazing how that large animal gets in and out. Notice the paws of the front legs which are bent against the body. They will pull the fox out. The hind legs trail in the tunnel. They will push the fox's body forward.

Lucky, the yankoo reporter, gave me a picture of that Red Fox. Here, I have it in my mail pouch.

It's a beautiful animal. In our forest we also have Gray Fox. The Red Fox fur color differs from that of the Gray Fox. Also, the tip of that bushy tail is white in the Red Fox. The tip of the bushy tail is black in the Gray Fox. That fox looks a lot like a dog, doesn't it, my friend? But that bushy tail especially says it's a fox. A dog doesn't have a bushy tail.

Both the Red and Gray Fox are night animals. They move about at night; they sleep in their den during the day. However, the Red Fox can also move about during the day.

See, there goes that Red Fox. It is checking out the hole in that tree trunk.

I hope it is not on the trail of Jiminy. Jiminy is a rabbit, and foxes like a rabbit meal. The yankoos have taken a liking to Jiminy. We will probably see Jiminy on our mail route. Jiminy visits the yankoo houses on a regular basis.

Oh, look over there, my friend. See that large insect on that tree trunk? That is a **Polyphemus Moth.** It is one of the largest moths found in our forest.

Finian, our yankoo naturalist, has studied the forest moths. He found the Polyphemus Moth caterpillars eating leaves of the oak, hickory, elm, and birch trees in our forest. Later, we shall meet Finian on the mail route.

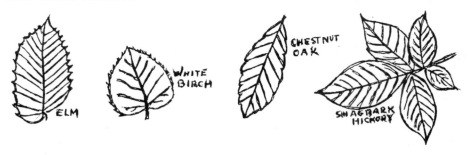

ELM

WHITE BIRCH

CHESTNUT OAK

SHAGBARK HICKORY

Let's get a little closer. I don't think the moth will fly away.

There, isn't that moth pretty? That is a female Polyphemus Moth. Notice, my friend, the moth has two pairs of wings. One pair is practically covering the second pair. Many animals would not notice that moth. Its color blends in well with the tree trunk. If an animal did spot the moth, it would be in for quite a scare. We won't disturb that moth on the tree though.

Here, let me sketch what the scare would be.

Notice one pair of wings covers the second pair. This allows the moth to blend in with the background. Now, let's say an animal comes closer.

Quick as a wink - the top wing moves up. Two large "eyes" suddenly stare at the animal. That is enough to scare most animals away. This eye-spot coloration is a protective feature of the moth. Many animals of the forest are colored for protection. Some blend in; so they won't be noticed. Some scare other animals by their coloration as this Polyphemus Moth does.

Now let's cross this small stream.

This stream is called Ben's Branch by the yankoos. Ben was one of the original forest yankoos. One could always find Ben fishing along this stream. Water runs in this stream all year. Often, especially in the springtime, water flows over the stream banks. The water stays in these low areas on the side of the stream. The area is a wetland. In this wetland area, one finds special plants. These plants do well in soil soaked with water. For example, Red Maples do well in these swampy areas.

Notice how much of the ground on this side of the stream is very wet.

Look at those plants there. My friend, those are Skunk Cabbage plants. They love the wet swampy area.

Early in the spring, the Skunk Cabbage produces its flower. After the flower is mature, the plant produces leaves. This is rather unusual for plants, my friend. Most plants produce leaves first and later on the flowers.

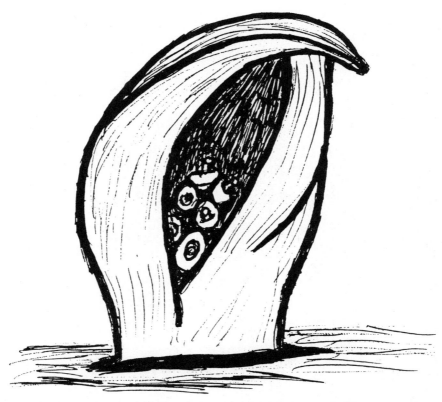

Here is a sketch I made of the flower. The cream-colored flower parts are inside the darker-colored covering. Skunk Cabbage is a very appropriate name. The flower odor resembles the spray odor of a skunk. But it pays to advertise. Very few insects are up and about in early spring. The insects must pollinate the flower. The odor will attract the insects. They come to obtain the nectar of the flower. In securing the nectar, they pollinate the flower.

After the flower is mature, the leaves come up. The leaves are large cabbage-like, as you can see in that plant there.

The cabbage-like leaves make plant food. This is stored in the stem and roots in the ground. When cold weather comes, the Skunk Cabbage leaves will die. What is left is underground. Come spring, the stored food will be used in making the flower. Then. the food will make the leaves of the plant.

Well, let's be on our way to Bruno's.

Oh, my friend, look at that butterfly. See, it has settled on that dead tree trunk. That is a Spicebush Swallowtail butterfly. Notice the tail-like projections from the hind wings. Butterflies with those projections are called Swallowtails. This is a common butterfly in our woods. It flies rather close to the ground as it goes along. Well, there it goes again on its way through the woods.

My friend, look at this tree over here. Notice the trough-like line going up that tree trunk. It appears quite different from the bark covered areas. That tree, my friend, has been struck by lightning. Whenever one sees such a line going up on a tree like that, one knows it has been hit by lightning.

This was the tallest tree in this area. A lightning bolt hit it. The electricity charge moved down the trunk to the ground. Going down, it stripped off the bark layer of the trunk. Small branches with leaves were also stripped from the tree trunk.

Once this has happened, no new bark will be laid down in that area. Instead, the tree covers the area with new wood. One could call this scar wood. It looks quite different from the bark covering. One can always recognize trees that have been hit by lightning. All will show this scar wood covering as we see in that tree.

CHAPTER TWO

BRUNO - THE YANKOO BAKER

Bruno, the yankoo baker, is at his bakery. Notice his gingerbread cookies, the yankoo, and clan size loaves of bread. The Blue Jay can usually be found in the tree by the bakery. That Blue Jay knows where good tasting food can be found.

Here comes Bruno. Just look, my friend, he is carrying a cake with some lighted candles on it.

"Happy Birthday, Lester! Happy Birthday, Lester! Look at the nice birthday cake I baked for you. See all those candles that are lighted? There are ten candles on that cake. They are for the ten years that you have delivered the mail. All the forest yankoos thank you. Day after day you bring us our mail."

Thank you, Bruno, thank you! I didn't know you knew my birth date. Indeed, you are right; today is my birthday.

That is a wonderful cake you have made for me. We will have to share it with the yankoos on my mail route. You know, my friend, we yankoos share things with one another.

Will they be surprised to find a mailman also delivering a piece of cake! Ten candles...I do declare...I didn't think it had been ten years that I have been delivering mail. When one loves his work, ten years can really fly by in a hurry.

You know, Bruno, I have enjoyed being the Yankoo mailman. Every day I look forward to meeting the yankoos. They are always happy. It makes me happy, too. You know, happiness is catching. We yankoos catch it from one another.

Oh, Bruno, meet my friend here. He is a friend of Olaf. He wants to learn more about our forest yankoos. Perhaps, you could tell him what life is like as a yankoo baker.   Why, Lester, I would be glad to tell him about the life of a yankoo baker. Everyday, I bake bread for the forest yankoos.

My bakery sign also lists all the pastries I bake for the yankoos.

Not all of these items are made each day. Oh, no, no! To make all of these would take a baker several 24-hour days. Besides, some berry pastries can only be made when the wild berries are ripe. Notice, my sign says that some items can only be made in season. All yankoos must order their bakery items the day before they are needed. That is what my sign says. I insist on this with the yankoos. In life, one must learn to look ahead. The yankoos are very good. They all put in their orders the day before. I guess I have trained them well in this regard. Once I know what the yankoos need, I can plan the baking schedule for that day.

So, every morning I get up early. I put on my baker's clothes. Now, I am ready for the day's work. I always bake the bread first. All the yankoos have to have bread at their meals.

Bread is a very important yankoo food. The pastries can come later. The bread must be well on its way before I begin anything else. I first check all the yankoo requests for regular yankoo loaves. I add up the number of yankoo loaves ordered. From experience, I know how much flour is needed to make a yankoo loaf. I multiply the amount of flour by the number of loaves needed. This gives me the amount of flour for yankoo loaves.

Next, I add up the number of clan size loaves ordered. I also know how much flour is needed to make a clan size loaf. So, here, too, I figure out the total amount of flour needed for all the clan size loaves. I next add these two amounts together, and I have the total flour needed.

Now, to the mixing bowl. I have a large mixing bowl in my bakery. Into the bowl goes the whole wheat flour and the other ingredients. To make yankoo bread tasty, I must admit that I add a little bit of honey to the dough. I mix the materials well.

Then I set it aside and cover it with a cloth. In about a half hour, the dough will rise to about twice the original size. In the meantime, I will work on the doughnuts and muffins the yankoos ordered. Then, back again to the bread. I now put it in pans. Once again, I let it rise for about 40 minutes; then, into the oven it goes.

Here are two pictures showing some of my loaves of bread. Lucky, the reporter for the Yankoo Gazette, took these pictures last week. He is writing a story on the bakery for his paper.

This picture shows a number of the regular loaves. We call these loaves the yankoo loaves.

Most yankoos use one yankoo loaf every two days.

Here is the other picture.

On that large leaf platter is a clan-size loaf. I make these clan-size loaves as needed. Yesterday, Ichabod ordered one. He will pick it up this afternoon. Tomorrow, he is having a fishing day at the stream for a group of yankoos. This loaf will take care of the bread needs of that yankoo group.

While the bread is baking, I start working on other items the yankoos ordered. The doughnuts and muffins are first prepared for baking. Then, I make cakes and pies that the yankoos need. After I have those taken care of, I work on some yankoo cookies.

Here is a picture of some gingerbread cookies that I made. It shows the large and small gingerbread cookies.

As you can see, those are mighty big gingerbread cookies. The young yankoos like a large size in their cookies. They had often told me that my cookies were just too small. They said, "Bruno, it takes an awful lot of your small cookies to fill us up. Why don't you make us some large cookies? Then we wouldn't have to eat so many to be filled up." Well, for some time I thought about this request from the young yankoos. I decided, after some thought, that the young yankoos were right.

If I made large cookies, they would not have to eat so many cookies. Then, too, if I made large cookies, it would be easier on the baker.

Making a few large cookies is much easier than making lots of small cookies. So, I told these young yankoos, "You are right, I should make large cookies for you. But if I do make these large cookies for you, you must eat every bit of a cookie you start eating. You cannot eat only part and throw away the rest of the cookie. If that happens, you get no cookies at all." You know, the young yankoos have been very good. They only have a small yankoo stomach. One large cookie I have found fills up that small stomach. I make sure they eat the whole cookie. I make those cookies tasty. A young yankoo will eat every bit of my large cookie.

All the yankoos of the forest help me in securing the materials I need to bake for them. When the berry season comes, they go out and harvest the berries for their pastries.

Blackberries

In the late summer and fall, they see that I get enough of the forest crab apples. And when the frost comes, they go out and climb the persimmon trees for the fruit. They have to wait until the frost or the persimmon would be quite tart. After a good frost though, the persimmon fruit becomes sweeter. However, the yankoos must get to the trees right away. Many other forest animals love the persimmons. Once a possum finds the tree after a frost, the tree will be stripped of persimmons. Possums love persimmons. Some yankoos have found wild wheat and corn plants in our forest.

They see to it that I have enough materials to make flour for my bakery goods You must realize, we yankoos help one another. What is life if all we think of is ourselves? No, we must think of others in life. We yankoos do. All the yankoos help one another.

So, I supply the forest yankoos with their bread and their sweets. The yankoos eat sweets in moderation. As you may have noted, so many of them are round enough. Of course, I admit that I pamper them at times. Once in a while, a yankoo is down and out. Then, I make sure he gets a tasty morsel to restore his spirits.

DOWN AND OUT YOUNG YANKOO + GINGER BREAD COOKIE = HAPPY YOUNG YANKOO

I love my job as the baker. Just think, every day I am helping supply food to all the forest yankoos. They all depend on me doing the baking. I must be dependable. I can't let them down. Every day I bake up some good pastries and bread to make the yankoos happy in their lives.

That, my friend, is what I, Bruno the baker, do. I enjoy every minute of it. Life is very worthwhile, my friend, when you really enjoy your work.

Well, I must get back to work. It was nice meeting you. We'll see you, Lester. Don't give away all of that cake. Eat a piece of it, at least. Goodbye now!

Oh, Bruno, here's your letter from Gilroy. Thanks again for the cake, Bruno. Well, my friend, we must be on our way. We have more yankoo mail to deliver.

CHAPTER THREE

LESTER, ON HIS MAIL ROUTE, MEETS
FINIAN - THE YANKOO NATURALIST

Lester and Finian check out some early spring flowers of the forest. The pink Bouncing Bet flowers and several kinds of violets are now in bloom. They grow along the edges of the forest.

Well, my friend, now we have a cake to take along on our mail route. Let's take the candles off the cake. There, now we can carry it along with us.

As we go along, we will give each yankoo a piece of cake. That was very thoughtful of Bruno. I didn't think he knew it was my birthday. But, you know, that was like Bruno. He always thinks about others. We need persons like Bruno, persons that are considerate of others. All the yankoos on our route will be happy to receive a piece of cake. They all love Bruno's pastries.

Now, let me look in my mail pouch. Smiley is the next yankoo on my route. I do believe that I have a letter for him today.

Yes, here it is, a postcard to Smiley from Oswald and Otis.

Otis and Oswald live in the Desert Region. They have their own mine. They are prospecting for gold. You can see that they are twins. They are pictured in front of their mine which is in the background. Their mine is called the Vulture Gold Mine. Notice their sign. It has a picture of the vulture found by their mine.

Oh, look over there, my friend. Do you see that butterfly? It just flew by us. It has rested on that piece of bark on the ground.

See the dark brown color of most of the wings? Then, notice the yellow margins on the wings. It also has bright blue spots next to the yellow margin. That is a beautiful butterfly. It is the very first butterfly we see in the forest every spring. It is called the Mourning Cloak butterfly.

This butterfly spends the winter here as an adult butterfly. This is very unusual. Most insects of the forest spend the winter in the egg or in the wormlike stage.

In late fall when winter approaches, this butterfly looks for a hollow in a tree. It spends the entire winter there as if it were "sleeping." As the temperature in the hollow rises and falls, so does the temperature of the butterfly. Spending the winter "sleeping" in this fashion is called hibernation.

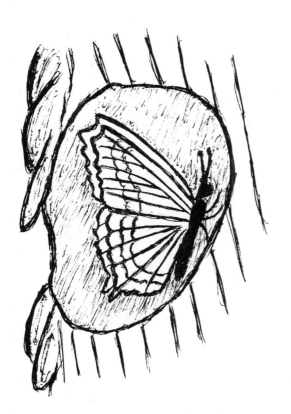

As spring approaches, with some warm days, the butterfly comes out of the hollow. It will spread its wings so that the rays of the sun will warm them. Until it warms up, it cannot fly.

The Mourning Cloak places its wings at a 45 degree angle to the sun's rays.

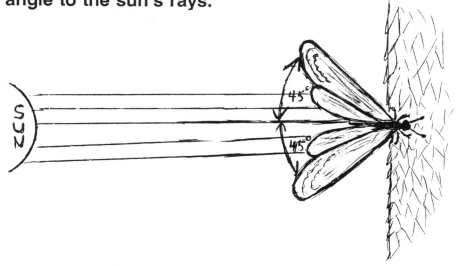

This produces rapid warming for this butterfly. Other butterflies hold their wings at other angles to the sun's rays. Some butterflies even let the sun's rays fall on the underside of their wings. Once the temperature of its body has risen, it will begin to fly.

Why, that looks like Finian over there. Do you see that yankoo with his magnifying glass in his hand? He is looking at something over there on the ground.

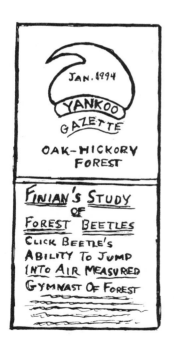

That is Finian. He is the yankoo naturalist. Finian studies all the plants and animals of the forest. His observations on forest life are published in the yankoo paper, the Yankoo Gazette.

He sees us. He is coming over to us. Hi Finian! What are you observing today?

Hi, Lester! Well, Lester, I have been watching that male Mourning Cloak butterfly. I believe you and your friend were also observing it. By the way, Lester, who is your friend? Oh, pardon me, this is Olaf's friend. He is going with me on my mail route. He wants to know more about our forest and the yankoos. Glad to meet you, my friend.

Lester, I am just completing a study of the life history of that Mourning Cloak butterfly. I have observed it many times for the past five years. Lester, I am going to give you a peek at part of it. The Yankoo Gazette will be publishing my observations in the summer.

Here, let me take out several drawings I have made. This is an egg mass laid by the female Mourning Cloak butterfly.

There are many, many eggs. The eggs encircle the branch. The female Mourning Cloak butterfly only lays the egg masses on certain trees. I have found them on the willow and ash tree branches in our forest.

WILLOW LEAF

ASH LEAF

So, the female butterfly knows the forest trees, too. Laying eggs on branches of oak and hickory trees wouldn't work. The caterpillars won't eat the leaves of these trees. The female butterfly knows on which trees to lay the egg masses.

The eggs hatch into small black colored caterpillars. The new leaves of the spring season are right there on the branch. Caterpillars grow fast. They spend practically all day eating leaves.

With all that eating every day, they reach a mature stage rather quickly. Here is a drawing I made of some caterpillars on a willow branch.   The caterpillars are black in color with some white spots here and there. Orange-red spots run lengthwise on the caterpillar's back.

The caterpillar then spins some strong threads and cements its hind end to the branch. Hanging head down, it now changes its shape.

Here is the sketch of this stage. It is called the chrysalis stage. Now, amazing things happen in the chrysalis.

All the caterpillar parts are broken down. New parts are being made. A new butterfly is being made. See, from the sketch, the very small wing being formed? It is absolutely magical. Here, a not-too-beautiful caterpillar is being made into a beautiful butterfly.

When the butterfly is completely formed, it breaks the thin cover. It climbs out of the chrysalis cover. Next, it pumps liquid into the empty wing tubes. This causes the folded wings to extend outward. When all the wings are extended, the butterfly is ready to fly.

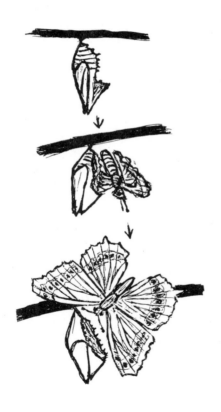

My friend, butterflies do not have to learn how to fly. No. No. They are expert flyers when they come out of the chrysalis. It is quite different with young yankoos and young yankees. They must first learn how to crawl. Then, they learn next how to walk. These butterflies start life with the ability to fly. Once their wings are extended, off they fly.

Lester, I have also made some studies on the food of this butterfly. The Mourning Cloak butterflies prefer nectar from milkweed, pussy willow, and daisy flowers. Even with other flowers around, it will visit flowers of one of these plants first.

All butterflies, like the spiders, eat only liquid food.

Butterflies do not have a mouth with teeth, as found in many animals. The butterfly has instead a long tube. This long tube is coiled up where a mouth would normally be in an animal.

When the butterfly goes to the milkweed flower, it uncoils this tube. The open end of the tube is placed down deep inside the flower in the pool of nectar. It then sucks up the nectar through the tube. It's like a young yankoo using a straw to drink its fruit juice.

Here is a sketch I have made that shows the long butterfly tube.

You know, Lester, the life history of a butterfly is amazing. An egg makes a not-too-beautiful caterpillar. The caterpillar turns into a chrysalis. A butterfly comes out of the chrysalis. Among the birds, an egg hatches into that bird. The chipmunks produce chipmunks. So to have this caterpillar become a beautiful butterfly is amazing. These sketches will be appearing in an article in the Yankoo Gazette.

I do believe I have taken up too much of your time, Lester. I know you have many letters to deliver.

Finian, we enjoyed learning about your observations. I am sure my friend has also learned much about this butterfly's life history. By the way, Finian, would you like a piece of cake? Bruno baked this cake for me. I would be happy if you accepted a piece of my cake.

Well, Lester, I appreciate your offer. No yankoo in our forest would refuse a piece of cake that Bruno baked. His cakes are delicious. I should know because I have eaten many of them. I am afraid that my love of pastries shows. I have a rather rounded-out figure. Yes, I would love a piece of your cake.

THAT'S BRUNO'S CAKE!

There, I have it. One bite now of the cake. Yes, that is one of Bruno's cakes. It is just delicious.

Thanks for the cake, Lester. I will be seeing you. Good bye, my friend. Good bye, Finian! Thanks for the advanced peek into your findings on the Mourning Cloak butterfly. We will look forward to reading the article in the Yankoo Gazette.

Well, my friend, let's continue on the mail route.

Oh, look at that bird nest, my friend. The wind must have blown it off the tree branch. We had some strong winds last night. Looking around, I don't see any eggs or young on the ground. So, that nest must have been empty.

Notice how well constructed that nest is. The bird must have spent some time making that nest. You know, my friend, all birds do not make the same kind of nest. Oh, no. Our forest Robin makes one kind of nest. The Catbird makes another type of nest. Each kind of bird makes its own characteristic nest. A bird is born with the "know-how" on making its nest. A bird does not have to learn how to make its nest.

Last year I took this picture of the dove on the nest. Notice how well the dove blends in with the leaves. As you can see, it's not too fancy a nest. It's really a lot of twigs arranged loosely into a platform.

The doves of our forest migrate south for the winter. The winter weather here is too cold for them. These flocks of doves settle down where it is warm and food is available. Then when spring arrives, they come back to our forest.

The male dove selects an area of the forest as its own territory. The pair then set about building a nest. The nest is usually in a crotch or on a branch of a tree. I have watched them build their nest. The male brings the twigs to the female at the nest site. The female arranges the twigs into the platform nest. After mating, the female will lay two white eggs. Last year, two broods were raised on this nest. This year, my friend, that same pair of doves is nesting over in this tree.

Notice, the dove is sitting on the eggs. The eggs must be kept warm. After about fourteen days, they will hatch into young doves. Once they have the young, then work really begins for the male and female. Doves only eat seeds. So, both male and female scour their territory for seeds for the young. As the young grow in size, they need more and more seeds. To ensure that they have enough seeds for the young, they drive all other doves out of their territory. One can hear their mournful sounds from dawn to dusk. It is a rather sad sounding "coo" "coo." This is really a warning to other doves. It says this land is taken. Keep out. The seeds here are ours.

Did you see that butterfly, my friend? See, it has settled down on that sassafras leaf in that sunny spot. That butterfly is the Silver-Spotted Skipper.

These butterflies are very fast fliers. The female butterflies lay their eggs on the leaves of the forest Black Locust tree. Most butterflies have antennae that are clubbed at the end. The skippers have sickle-shaped antennae. These antennae, it is believed, help the butterfly sense odors. The skippers have long proboscis tubes. They drink the nectar from the flower base area. To reach these nectar pools, they must have a long proboscis.

CHAPTER FOUR

SMILEY AND REGINALD - THE YANKOO LIQUID SUPPLIERS

These are the yankoo liquid suppliers. Notice Smiley has a yankoo bottle of Ginger Ale. Reginald has a yankoo bottle of Big Pool Spring Water. Supplying liquids to the forest yankoos keeps both Smiley and Reginald very busy. They like their work. They are helping other yankoos.

Smiley and Reginald live just around those large bushes. See, Smiley is over there by his sign. Now, I do believe that he has heard us coming. Yes, he is coming toward us now.

Hi Lester!

How are you?

Hi Smiley! Oh, I am fine today. Who is your friend, Lester? My friend knows Olaf, the postmaster. Olaf has asked me to take him along while I deliver today's mail. He is very interested in learning more about our forest and the yankoos.

Glad to meet you, my friend. I am sure Lester will point out many wonders of our forest. He also will tell you about the forest yankoos.

Do you have a letter for me today, Lester? Yes, Smiley, here is a postcard for you. It is from Otis and Oswald. Oh, good, I have been wondering how Oswald and Otis are doing out there in the Rocky Mountains.

What do you think of my sign, Lester?

Smiley, you have made a real artistic sign; I like it.

Well, I am proud of that sign. I have just put the finishing touches on it. As you can see, the overall shape is rather unusual. That is the shape of our yankoo bottles, my friend. I hear that you yankees have another name for our yankoo bottles. They tell me the yankees call our yankoo bottles, gourds.

What was that, my friend? Oh, you wonder where one finds these yankoo bottles in the forest? Well, there is a story behind these yankoo bottles. We yankoos are indebted to a yankee farmer for our yankoo bottles. Years ago, a yankee farmer planted a garden alongside our forest. He grew all kinds of vegetables in his garden.

When I was over in that area of the forest, I would look at his garden. He grew many kinds of vegetables, and they were all healthy plants. His squash plants intrigued me.

The yankee farmer made small hills of dirt. He planted seeds in the tops of these hills. The seeds produced many vines. As these vines grew, they fell down to the ground. They then branched and branched, making a wide carpet of branches with leaves. The squash vines produced many flowers that attracted the honey bees. In seeking the nectar of the flowers, the bees pollinated the flowers. Each pollinated flower then changed into a squash. The farmer harvested the squash when the outside skin was tender.

One fall day over ten years ago, I was hiking with some other yankoos over in that area. We went to look at the yankee garden and found it overgrown with weeds. The yankee farmer had given up gardening.

I picked up a squash that was lying on the ground. The squash had dried out and was very light in weight. The outside covering had become quite hard. I told the other yankoos that these might make good containers for my liquids. So, we picked up a number of these dried-out squash and took them back to the forest.

Once I had them back at my shop, I cut off the top of the neck of each squash. I turned each one upside down, and the seeds dropped out. I set all these seeds aside. Next, I washed each squash inside and out. Then I filled each one with our spring water. They all held the water. Not a drop of water leaked from any of the squash.

Next, I put a stopper at the neck end of each squash. Then, I dropped each water-filled squash on

the ground. None of the squash broke! None of the water spilled out! "Glory be!" I yelled. "I have discovered the yankoo bottle."

I tell you that was so loud, I was sure every yankoo in the forest heard it. Just think, here I had discovered the yankoo bottle. I could fill it with our spring water. The bottle does not leak and, if dropped, it does not break. Here was the ideal yankoo bottle. You remember, don't you, Lester, what things were like before the yankoo bottle? Every day each forest yankoo had to go to the Big Pool and get the day's water. Now, they wouldn't have to do that anymore. I could deliver several yankoo bottles of spring water to every yankoo. It would last for several days.

Oh, I tell you, we forest yankoos are indeed indebted to that yankee farmer. If he had not planted that garden by our forest, we might never have had these wonderful yankoo bottles.

Look at my rack of yankoo bottles over there. That's our supply on hand-to-deliver-our-spring water and my squeesins. Every year we plant squash seed in that abandoned garden. Every year we harvest the dried-out squash. We have two different kinds of bottles. One kind has straight necks. The other kind has crooked necks. Notice on my stand a third kind on the bottom shelf. I found these two in the garden last year. They hold a little more liquid than the other two kinds.

Oh, yes, I almost forgot to tell you about the stoppers for these yankoo bottles. Several yankoos found some large acorns that fit some bottles. These yankoos whittled some hickory nuts into the right shape as stoppers for the larger yankoo bottle openings.

So, you see, we do have enough yankoo bottles for our spring water and my squeesins.

The most popular "squeesin" is my ginger ale. The yankoos work hard each day. When they get a little tired, they have a drink of my ginger ale. They say it peps them up. Then back to work they go.

Smiley in Crab Apple tree checking out the flowers.

Smiley checking out fall crop of crab apples.

In the fall, the yankoos collect the crab apples on the trees alongside the edge of the forest. From my squeesins, I get a tasty crab apple juice. The yankoos love crab apple juice. Some of this juice I keep and make into vinegar. You know, the yankoos like a little vinegar to pep up their salads. Some of the crab apple crop goes to Pierre. Pierre is the chef at the Yankoo Eatery. He makes apple butter from some of the apple crop. Pierre also makes all the jams for the yankoos. From my squeesins, I also make grape and huckleberry juice; and Pierre makes jams from the rest of the crop.

Here comes Reginald. Hi Reginald! We have a guest here, Reginald. He is going with Lester on his mail route. Hello, my friend. I have to deliver this bottle of spring water to Gramps. I just received word that he has run out of water. So, if you will excuse me, I must hurry to Gramps. Enjoy your visit with our yankoos. Good bye!

Well, Lester, there goes Reginald. He is so eager. He is a very valuable helper. When he does something for me, I can depend on it being done right. Right now, he is handling all the spring water deliveries to the forest yankoos. I am busy with my squeesins at this time.

You know, Lester, Reginald has certainly changed. My friend, Reginald, used to worry a lot. Here, let me show you this picture I took of him last fall.

Here it is. See, he was really a worrisome yankoo. He worried about everything. Well, we finally said, "Gramps, why don't you help Reginald? He is a worry wart." Well, Gramps had Reginald over; he talked with him; and now Reginald hasn't a worry in the world. He is entirely different. We owe it all to Gramps. Gramps is one of our oldest forest yankoos, my friend. He has experienced much in his life. He has learned from his experiences. He is wise in the art of living. He helps all the yankoos when they have problems. He has certainly helped our Reginald. Smiley, have a piece of my birthday cake. Bruno baked it for me. You won't have to ask me a second time, Lester. I like Bruno's cakes.

Oh, it tastes good. Thank you, Lester. You should have a birthday cake every day.

Well, I must get back to my squeesins. It has been nice meeting you, my friend. Come back again some time. Good bye, Lester. Thanks for the postcard and the cake!

CHAPTER FIVE

LESTER - ON HIS MAIL ROUTE

The Eastern Box turtle passes Lester on his mail route. During hot, dry weather, the box turtles keep cool by burrowing under logs in the forest.

Look over there on the leaves of that branch, my friend. Do you see that large insect?

It's green in color. Notice how it blends in with the color of those green leaves. It is not moving. Being colored like the leaves and not moving help keep it alive. Many animals that would eat it don't notice it. Blending in with the leaves and not moving also help it secure food. Other insects do not notice it until it is too late.

The Praying Mantis walks on leaves looking for insects. It has wings and can also fly from one plant to another plant.

As you can see, it is a rather large insect. It is about three inches long. Notice that it has six legs. Four legs do the walking. Those front legs are modified into pincers for catching insects. They are not used for walking. Notice how this pair is bent backwards towards the insect body. See how the ends of these legs are held close together, in a "praying" manner. That, my friend, gives the insect its name, Praying Mantis.

If an insect comes within range of those front legs, it will be caught. "Quick as a wink" those front legs go out and catch the insect. The forelegs then bring the insect back to its mouth. The Praying Mantis will then bite off parts. It will eat that insect piece by piece.

In autumn, the female Praying Mantis lays hundreds of eggs on a twig. The eggs are covered by a soft, frothy mass that quickly hardens. Very few animals bother this egg mass. The egg mass passes through the wintertime and then the eggs hatch the next spring. Each egg is in a separate chamber inside this egg mass. When spring comes, the egg will have changed into a young mantid. The young mantid cuts out an opening to the outside. Now, it searches for food. Mantids have quite an appetite. They will eat most any insect they encounter. Sometimes, they even eat other mantids. The mouth parts are very strong, and they cut right through the hard covering of the insects.

Remember, my friend, how Finian examined the life cycle of the Mourning Cloak butterfly? The butterfly had an egg, caterpillar, chrysalis and adult stage in its life. Well, the Praying Mantis life cycle is rather simple compared to that butterfly life cycle.

The Praying Mantis egg hatches into a very small mantid. It looks just like an adult mantid. As it eats more and more insects, it grows larger and larger. Finally, it is as large as it will ever become. It is an adult, about three inches or more in length. So, young mantids hatching from the eggs look just like adults, except for their smaller size.

Most insects have their heads attached directly to the next part of the body. Look at that Squash Bug. Notice how the head is attached to its body. It has no neck.

Most insects are built like that Squash Bug. They have no neck. To turn the head, the insect must move the whole body.

The Praying Mantis has a neck. It can turn its head to the right and the left, without moving its body. This is very helpful when it comes to catching nearby insects. Slowly turning the head does not alarm an insect. Moving the whole mantid body would cause an insect to quickly fly away.

The Praying Mantis, my friend, is a very beneficial insect. It eats many of our forest insects. It helps keep a good balance in insect numbers. Well, let's be on our way. We have more letters to deliver.

Look over there at that tree, my friend. Do you see that vine on the bark of that tree? That vine is the Poison Ivy vine. It is a plant that we yankoos do not touch. All parts of that vine produce a poisonous substance. Touching it can cause a rather painful skin irritation. As we yankoos say, "Leaflets in three - let them be." Notice the large leaves have three leaflets.

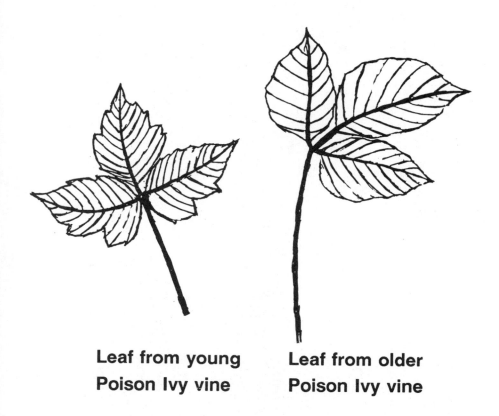

Leaf from young   **Leaf from older**
Poison Ivy vine   **Poison Ivy vine**

When the vine is small, the leaves have leaflets that are "toothed" as it were. Older leaves have leaflets that lack these indentations. Vines in nature often grow "piggy back" on another plant. The vine stem is too weak to hold itself up in the air. So it attaches itself to another plant. That Poison Ivy vine produces air roots that attach it firmly to the tree trunk. Now, without using much energy, it can grow right up the tree trunk.

The vine produces many white flowers. See them on that vine there? Once pollinated, the flowers produce white fruits. Inside each fruit is a seed.

Many of the forest birds eat these Poison Ivy fruits. The seed inside the fruit is not digested by the bird. The seed is cast out with the bird droppings.

The seed can now sprout in a new spot in the forest. Thus, the birds scatter the seed of the Poison Ivy vine in the forest. The birds received the fruit around the seed for doing this.

So you see, my friend, the Poison Ivy plant needs the birds. The birds need the fruit of the Poison Ivy plant as food.

Oh, oh, let's stop here. See that sunny spot ahead? A very large Black Snake is sunning itself there. Let's move slowly towards it.

That is a big Black Snake. It must be over five feet long. It is warming itself there in that sunny spot. Snakes have to get warmed up every morning. Their body temperature is always the temperature of the surrounding area. So, if it is cold, the snake is cold. Birds and higher animals have set temperatures. These animals stay warm even though it is cold around them. So, when it is cold, the snake hides. When it becomes warm, the snake becomes warm. Then it becomes active. Snakes often warm up in the sun as this Black Snake is doing.

That Black Snake can move very fast. It catches rats, mice, rabbits, chipmunks and other small animals. The snake will throw body coils around an

animal. This happens very quickly. The Black Snake holds the animal in a coil. Then it pushes the animal against the ground, suffocating it. Once the animal is dead, the snake will eat it.

Snakes have teeth which do not cut up the food they eat. They eat all of their food whole. They swallow the entire animal. Snakes have many teeth lining both the upper and lower jaws. All the teeth end in a very fine point, and all point backwards. These teeth help in swallowing the animal.

A snake has a very
unusual jaw setup.
It can swallow an
animal greater in
diameter than itself.
Most animals have one
solid bone in the
lower jaw. The snake
has two bones. The
bones are connected to
each other, in front,
by elastic tissue.

This allows the mouth opening to widen sideways as
it swallows a large animal.

Where the lower jaw
meets the skull, there
is another unusual setup.
The lower jaw, attached
to the skull, works like
two hinges. One hinge
allows the lower jaw to
stretch downward.

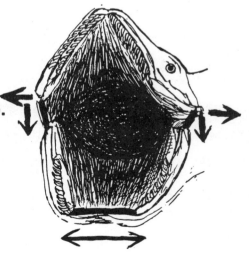

The other hinge arrangement allows the area to stretch sideways. This enables the snake to swallow an animal that is greater in diameter than the snake.

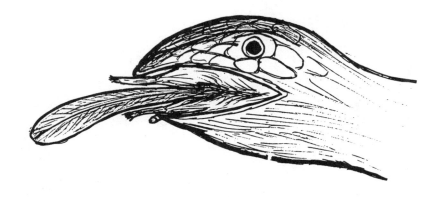

Snakes always swallow an animal head first. The head of an animal is usually smaller than the diameter of the body of the animal. The snake will grab the head first with its mouth. Then, slowly but surely, the jaw muscles will draw the animal through the mouth opening. When a larger part of the animal comes to the mouth, the mouth opening enlarges as it takes it in. The whole process of swallowing an animal takes some time. Once the animal is in the digestive system, it will be broken down. It takes a snake quite a few days or even weeks to entirely digest a larger animal.

Let's move a little closer to that Black Snake. Notice how the head draws back. It is off the ground. The body is thrown into a coil below the head. That is the characteristic defensive pose a snake takes. From this position the snake can strike some distance at an animal. Before an animal realizes it, the snake coils would wind around it. The speed with which the snake strikes is incredibly fast. "Quick as a wink" an animal is caught in the snake coils.

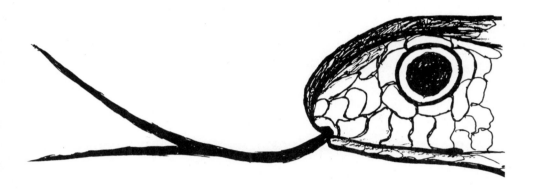

As you can see, that snake tongue is forked. The tongue flicks back and forth for a few seconds. Then, into the mouth it goes, another second, out comes the tongue again. The forks of that tongue pick up chemical odor particles in the air and on the ground. It transfers these particles to a structure in the roof of the mouth cavity. The nerves there take the information to the brain. Now the snake knows the kind of animal that left the odor trail. So a snake tracks its food, the prey, by using its tongue. The ability of the tongue to pick up odor particles also helps a snake find a mate. This ability also warns the snake about a nearby enemy, a predator.

You know, my friend, we need these snakes in our forest. The forest rats and mice produce many young each year. These rodents along with other small animals are the basic snake foods. At times, snakes will eat bird eggs and young birds.

No, we don't have to worry that there will be too many snakes in our forest. Skunks and raccoons eat snakes. Some snakes eat other snakes. The Broad-winged Hawk, Red-tailed Hawk, and Cooper's Hawk capture forest snakes during the day. At night the Great Horned Owl of the forest captures snakes and rodents. So, you see, we have a fine balance in the kinds and numbers of animals. We have an adequate number of each kind of forest animal. We do not have too many animals of any one kind in our forest.

Before we continue on our mail route, my friend, let's look at this plant over here. It is a Bloodroot plant. Bloodroot is one of the wild flowers that bloom early in the spring in the forest.

Oh, you wonder why such a name for a wild flower? Well, I must admit that it is a rather unusual name for a wild flower. However, when one learns a little more about the plant, the name seems to fit. The Bloodroot plant has a short, rather stubby root stock. If one cuts this root stock, a reddish liquid flows from it. This is a little unusual for plant roots. So, it seems that this plant's feature gave rise to the common name, Bloodroot.

I made these drawings to illustrate how the Bloodroot grows. The first sketch on the right shows an early stage. The plant grows, from the stem and root in the ground, up into the air. The leaf is curled up around the flower stalk. The flower head grows on this flower stalk inside the curled leaf. The middle drawing shows a slightly later stage in growth. Now, the leaf has uncurled. The third drawing shows the mature plant and flower. The single leaf of the plant is still growing in size. The flower has opened and has eight white petals. The flower parts in the center are bright yellow.

The mature flower is now above the shorter leaf. The flower opens in the morning and closes in the evening. It attracts bees and insects looking for its nectar. In securing the nectar, the insects also pollinate the flower. The flower then produces seeds and turns into a seed pod. The leaves continue to grow in size until mid-summer. By this time, each leaf can be nine inches wide and almost twelve inches long. The leaves are now producing food. This food will be used to build up the stubby root stalk again. All of the food that had been stored in the root stalk was used to produce this plant. Now, the root stalk is once again built up with stored food. This will be used next spring to make the Bloodroot plant. When the seeds have matured, the pod will break open. The seeds will spill on the ground. Next year, some of those seeds will grow into small Bloodroot plants.

Well, my friend, I must be leaving you, now. I hope that you will join me in Book Four. Along the mail route we should see more forest plants and animals. We will also deliver mail to Pierre who is the yankoo chef. He runs the Pierre Yankoo Eatery - Under Tall Oaks.

One never knows, we might meet Finian again. That yankoo naturalist is forever discovering interesting aspects about our forest plants and animals.

Then we will deliver mail to Gramps. He is the oldest yankoo in the forest.

Our mail route will also take us to Rufus' hut.

Rufus is our weather elf. He keeps us informed, day by day, on the kind of weather we can expect.

Along our mail route we might see Zephyr. He is always busy delivering packages to the forest yankoos.

Then we will make our way to where Methuselah lives. Methuselah is our yankoo ecologist who is a very intelligent yankoo. He is the "brainy" yankoo of our forest. I am sure he will tell us about some interesting aspects of our forest.

So, goodbye my friend. Join me again in Book Four, and we will deliver the mail together.

FOX

TRACKING IT DOWN

SKUNK

RACCOON

OPOSSUM

DEER

American Elves - The Yankoos

The Yankoos and the Oak-Hickory Forest Ecology

This is the third in the five book series on plant and animal life in a forest. These books, presenting the wonders of nature in a forest, make ideal gifts for children.

The following three books of the series are now available for purchase. Persons ordering books of the series will be notified when the final two books, now in preparation, are published.

Book One: Illustrated, 64 pages
Soft Cover, 6x9   Cost: $7.95 postpaid

Book Two: Illustrated, 96 pages
Soft Cover, 6x9   Cost: $7.95 postpaid

Book Three: Illustrated, 96 pages
Soft Cover, 6x9   Cost: $7.95 postpaid

Send orders for books to: Yankoo Publishing Co.
10616 W. Cameo Drive
Sun City, AZ 85351-2708

Make checks payable to: Yankoo Publishing Co.
Please allow two weeks for U.S. Postal Service delivery.